THE
LIGHTS
OF
DIWALI

Carol M. Hansen

Laurel Traye, Editor

 **FriesenPress**

Suite 300 – 990 Fort Street
Victoria, BC, Canada V8V 3K2
www.friesenpress.com

ISBN
978-1-4602-5512-4 (Hardcover)
978-1-4602-5513-1 (Paperback)
978-1-4602-5514-8 (eBook)

1. Juvenile Fiction, Fairy Tales & Folklore, Single Title

Distributed to the trade by The Ingram Book Company

TABLE
OF
CONTENTS

For my family,
especially for granddaughters
Abby and Juli,
and
remembering Shyam Mali

THE LIGHTS
OF DIWALI

Diwali, India's beloved festival of lights, occurs yearly, rotating between October and November. Indians look forward to this holiday wherever they live. It's fun. It's colorful and exciting. But the lights are more than fun. They symbolize the victory of light over dark, good over evil. This five-day festival springs from ancient religious traditions. One tradition honors Lakshmi, goddess of wealth and prosperity. It is said that she will visit homes where the inhabitants' hearts are pure and the houses are spotlessly clean. Another Diwali tradition is that of Lord Rama and his wife, Sita. Lights and celebration welcomed them home after an unfair fourteen-year banishment from the kingdom of Lord Rama's birth.

Today at Diwali, lights are everywhere—inside houses, around windows, over doors, and adorning buildings. Flickering lights send out beams that invite all people to celebrate.

This book is a fictional story that stars a fictional Indian family. It is set in a middle-sized city located in northwest India. A list of characters in the family appears below, followed by a list of major characters taken from the epic poem *Ramayana* (recapped in chapter seven).

INDIAN FAMILY MEMBERS IN THE STORY

Mona: ten years old; the conscience of her siblings (most of the time).

Mohan: aged twelve; a bit of a bully; skeptical; in the end, a caring brother.

Sunil: five years old; the family baby; wants to be big, to be accepted, and to be wise.

Papa: accountant for a local business; embraces the holiday exuberance of his children, and urges them toward understanding the heart of this popular festival.

Mum/Mummy: Chief Operations Officer of the home and everything in it.

Ram Lal: elderly live-in servant; widowed; dedicated to the family.

Dada: Grandfather; Papa's father.

Dadi: Grandmother; Papa's mother.

Sharma-*ji:* Papa's former boss (*"ji"* is an honorific that refers to an important or close friend).

Raj: Sharma's son; visiting from the U.S.

Lakshmi: Raj's new wife; named for the goddess Lakshmi.

CHARACTERS IN CHAPTER 7: FROM
THE EPIC POEM, RAMAYANA

The old king: ruler of A-yodh-ya; Rama's father.

His youngest queen: beautiful and scheming; mother of Bharata.

Rama: hero of the poem; heir to the throne.

Sita: Rama's devoted wife; beautiful and gentle.

Lakshman: Rama's younger brother; devoted to the royal couple.

Hanuman: monkey deity; strong, loyal, and powerful; friend to Rama.

Sugriva: king of the monkeys.

Ravana: demon king of Lanka, an island near India.

THE
LIGHTS
OF
DIWALI

CHAPTER 1

THE SECRET

Mona giggled behind her fingertips. Her eyes searched the courtyard and paused at the great tree by the wall of the family compound. "Shh, Mohan," she whispered. "Sunil's over there by the tree."

The tree's branches created a lacework of afternoon shadow, partially disguising a small boy. He stood quietly, watching and listening to his older siblings' intense conversation.

"So?" scoffed Mohan, the eldest. "He can't hear us, and besides ... what can he do about anything? Nobody listens to Sunil." Mohan stopped for a moment, and then continued with a lowered voice, looking toward the tree and Sunil. "Look, tomorrow is Diwali and I have a great plan. But it has to be a secret, just between us, or we'll be in trouble. Big Trouble."

Mona gasped. "I don't want trouble, Mohan," she protested.

Over by the tree, Sunil straightened, and a look of determination flashed in his eyes. He began to inch slowly forward, out of the tree's protective shadows.

Mona glanced toward him. She realized that he had, indeed, heard their words. Like it or not, Sunil would be part of the secret. She turned to Mohan. "Can we tell this secret to Papa and Mummy?"

"No! Then it's not a secret."

By now, Sunil was standing next to Mona. Silently, she reached down and took his hand in hers.

"That's exactly who we *can't* tell," continued Mohan. "And not *Dada*, or *Dadi* either. Nobody ... not even old Ram Lal! It's a secret. That's what a secret is. You don't tell anyone!" His eyes snapped from Mona to Sunil. "Maybe I'm sorry I even said anything to you."

"You haven't said anything yet, Mohan. You just said that you have a secret and we can't tell anyone. So, what is this secret?"

Mohan pulled a small box of matches from his pocket. Mona gasped as he waved it around. "What do you think these are for, Mona? They're part of the secret."

Mona wasn't sure she wanted to continue the conversation, but her curiosity was stronger than her caution. "I don't know. Do you have cigarettes too? Is that your big secret? Then you will be in trouble, Mohan. That's for sure."

"Do you think I'm stupid?" He glanced at Sunil. "I wouldn't tell you, or anybody else, if I had cigarettes ... would I?"

"Well . . ." offered Sunil tentatively.

The older boy barked at his little brother, "Well what, Sunil?" With that direct question, Mohan officially included his younger brother in the conversation.

"Mohan, stop that!" Mona countered. "Sunil just wants to know what you're talking about, and so do I. Are you going to tell us your secret, or not?"

"*Puh-TAH'-kay*, Mona! Fireworks! That's my secret." Mohan pocketed the matches and cast a smug look at his siblings.

"That's crazy, Mohan. You know we're not allowed to shoot fireworks." Sunil nodded vigorously and moved closer to Mona.

Ignoring them, Mohan continued. "We can shoot off puh-TAH'-kay tonight when no one's here. I happen to know that Mum is going over to Ved Uncle's house to make Diwali sweets with Dadi.

And Papa's working late so he can take off tomorrow." A wide grin reflected Mohan's excitement. "Since we're out of school for the holiday, I can go to market this afternoon," he said, pulling a fistful of money from a second pocket, "with this." Mona and Sunil sucked in air. Their jaws dropped in disbelief.

"Where did you get all that money?" Mona whirled and looked around the courtyard. No one was there. It was just the three of them. Her heart thumped in her chest and her stomach cramped. "Where did you get that money, Mohan?"

Mohan was twelve and Mona was ten. They each got an allowance, but not nearly so much as what Mohan had in his hand.

"I saved it, of course! What do you think? It's my allowance, and my birthday money ... and I earned some of it. Took me a long time." Mohan paused to look at the pile of rupees in his hand. "But I'll share. It wouldn't be any fun to shoot puh-TAH'-kay alone."

After a long pause, Mona giggled and said, "It *would* be fun!" As long as she could remember, she had seen neighbors enjoying shooting these special fireworks year after year. In her mind's eye, she could see small shooters writhing like little snakes, and others streaking over houses, and over their great tree, whistling as they leaped high into the night, sparkles bursting into colorful sky flowers. Her heart began to thump—this time with excitement. But she knew the family rule: No puh-TAH'-kay in this family. Ever!

Mohan's voice broke into her thoughts. "So! Here's my plan. I'll buy the puh-TAH'-kay now—this afternoon. We can shoot them tonight when we're alone."

"Ram Lal will be here. He'll catch us," countered Mona.

"So what if he catches us? He won't say anything, because if he does, he'll be in trouble with Papa for letting us do it."

Mona glanced at Sunil, who was standing beside her—his eyes huge and his look doubtful. "I-I-I don't know," she stammered. "Ram

Lal isn't scared of Papa. He's been with us forever. Besides, he's much older than Papa. Oh, he'll tell all right." Mona was sure of herself on that point. "Then what?" Sunil nodded again. Ram Lal wasn't afraid of Papa. No way!

Mohan was unmoved by this argument. "Ram Lal will be in the house, watching TV. You know he likes to do that when Mum and Papa are out. And besides, what can Papa do after we've already shot them? Take away our *Diwali* sweets?" He turned to his little brother. "That would be a good time for you to start crying, Sunil. You're good at that. Mum will be sorry for us and give some of the sweets back." Refusing to be discouraged, Mohan began to stamp out a little dance, chanting, "Puh-TAH'-kay, puh-TAH'-kay, put, put, put, puh-TAH'-kay!"

"Mohan, stop it!" ordered his sister.

Sunil's eyes glistened with tears. "I don't like puh-TAAK!" he burst out. "We have to tell Papa."

"Puh-tah'-**kay**'" corrected Mohan. "You don't even know how to say it."

"I do so! But why can't we tell anyone?"

"You wouldn't understand!"

"You think you're so smart," grumbled Sunil. He paused, and then withdrew his hand from Mona's grip, stood with his hands on his hips, and tried very hard to look fierce—and big. "I think I'll tell Papa that you have matches. Then you'll be in big trouble."

Mohan glared at him. "I'll just say that I found them. You're so stu—"

"Mohan!" snapped Mona. She saw a huge tear roll down Sunil's cheek. He was only five, after all, and really not so brave at all. She took his hand again. "You wouldn't tell on us, would you, Sunil?" she asked softly. "That would be mean. We wait all year for Diwali, and you could spoil it for all of us."

"Well," Sunil shuffled his feet, "maybe not ... but ..."

"All right, Sunil," stated Mohan grudgingly, "as long as you're in this with us, you'd better keep your mouth shut, or you'll be in trouble too."

Sunil said nothing. Waiting tears finally cascaded down his cheeks. Seeing this, Mona wiped at them with the heel of her open hand. She put her arm around his sagging shoulders and squarely faced the older boy. Mohan turned away, ignoring the tearful scene.

"I don't know, Mohan. This is kind of scary," ventured Mona. "And you're acting so important. Would shooting puh-TAH'-kay really be fun if it makes trouble for all of us? If it didn't have to be a secret, it could be just lots of fun." Mohan turned back, as she took a step forward, dragging Sunil with her. "We could ask Papa and Mummy if we could *pleeease* shoot puh-TAH'-kay this year. Couldn't we do that? We're not babies anymore, and Papa could do it with us."

Sunil turned to Mona. She caught his confused look. "What's the matter, *Bay-ta?*" He choked back a sob. It wasn't often that Mona called Sunil "Bay-ta" (a term of endearment), but he looked so small.

"I don't want to shoot puh-TAAK," he gulped. "It's scary."

"You don't have to be here, Sunil," comforted Mona. "You can ask to go to Uncle's house with Mummy. You can carry Mummy's basket. She'd like that. And think about the other things we do at Diwali. Think of the twinkly lights. Remember last year? You had such fun." Sunil nodded, fisting tears from his eyes, as Mona rattled on. "We walked down the middle of the road toward the market with Mummy and Papa. Lights were over our heads. They were strung from side to side over the street." Mona raised her arm and swayed back and forth, as though she were stringing lights. "They made a ceiling like millions of stars, and we walked along beneath them. Can you remember that, Sunil? Lights overhead, all the way to the market." Mona's arm waved a final grand arch, suggesting the family's arrival at their destination.

Sunil nodded again and smiled wanly. "Then we walked back to Uncle's house to say prayers and to eat some of Dadi's sweets. Papa even gave each of us some rupees to spend on something special." Sunil brightened at the thought of rupees in his pocket. He even popped his hand into a pocket and acted like he was jingling coins.

"I know, but ..."

Mohan interrupted. "It's still going to be a secret," he declared. "That's part of the fun, and besides, I'll do the shooting!" This silenced Sunil. He and Mona stood together, holding hands. They knew that Mohan was in charge, and that the plan was made!

CHAPTER 2

MORE
PLANS

The iron gate squeaked open. Mona turned to see Papa walking through into the courtyard. It was early. *"Wasn't Papa planning to stay late at work today?"* Mona thought. She swung around to her brothers, raising a questioning brow. Mohan shook his head ever so slightly. *Keep the secret!*

"Well, well, well ... what have we here? All three of my children in one place at the same time! I'm a lucky papa, but ..." he paused, "you look surprised."

Mona's stomach tightened. "We are surprised, Papa. We thought you were working late today." Had he heard their conversation as he approached the walled-in courtyard where they stood? She swallowed her fear and changed the subject.

"Papa, Diwali starts tomorrow," she burst out. "Did you get Mummy a new pot for the kitchen? We always do that."

"I will. We'll buy one together, but not yet," smiled her father. He kissed Sunil on the cheek and ran his hand across Mona's shiny black hair. Then he turned to his tall, sometimes rebellious, Mohan and gently gripped his shoulder. Papa walked toward the front door of the house and started up the three cement steps. Before entering the house, he turned and continued. "We need to talk." No one said anything.

After a pause, Mona asked, "Talk about what, Papa?" Her stomach knotted up again, because usually when Papa said those words, someone was in trouble. Were they in trouble? Could Papa possibly know about the secret? Had he, after all, been standing outside the wall, listening to their conversation?

Their father smiled patiently. "We need to talk now," he repeated, "about Diwali. I have a very good plan that I want to share with you." He paused for a moment and then continued. "I came home early especially for that reason." Scanning their puzzled faces, he continued. "Are you coming?"

The three children looked at each other. *"What is Papa's plan?"* thought Mona. She relaxed a little, though, because he didn't appear to know about the secret. He was too calm—almost jovial. And Papa said that he had a plan of his own. But if it was a special plan, a very good plan, what could it be? Her imagination went to work and sent her mind spinning. *"Could Papa's plan be anything like Mohan's?"* No, it couldn't be. Their family had never before shot puh-TAH'-kay, so why would he permit it now, all of a sudden? Mona decided to wait and see.

"Come on into the house with me," coaxed their father. "We'll ask Mum to make us some tea. Then we can talk." He started through the door. The children stood like statues. "Come on," said Papa, looking puzzled. "Come on. We'll talk."

"Will Mummy talk to us too?" asked Sunil. "Does Mummy have a plan?" He cast a look at his brother and sister. Then he stood up straight. "We have a plan, Papa," he announced loudly. Mona and Mohan exchanged alarmed glances.

"Oh?" said Papa. "You have a plan too?" He paused, then captured each child's attention with a riveting glance, and said, "I want to tell you about my plan first." His face expanded with a conspiratorial grin. It wouldn't have surprised Mona if he had broken into a little Papa dance, right there in the doorway.

"But to answer your question, Sunil, no ... your mum doesn't have a plan. Not that I know of anyway. Part of my plan is for her, but a special part is for you children, for me, and for Dada ... even for Ram Lal. That special part isn't for Mum or Dadi. It's just for us." Papa's smile suggested a super secret of his own. "Do you want to talk about it, or don't you?"

"I do!" blurted Sunil. "I want to tell you about our plan." Mona stomped on Sunil's foot.

"Ouch!" cried the little boy.

"Well be quiet and let Papa talk," warned Mona.

"Yes," said Papa. "I'll talk first. Then you can tell me about your plan."

"Ours isn't much," murmured Mohan.

"Oh yes it is," Sunil sang out. He started to say more, but a withering look from Mohan stopped him short.

Papa hadn't witnessed the exchange anyway. He was already in the kitchen talking to Mum, asking for tea for himself and for the three children. Mona knew that her papa enjoyed times like this—time to sit and talk with his family. Little did she know, though, how special this talk was going to be. It was just for himself and for the children.

Mona liked the cozy sitting-and-talking times with her papa, although they got a little boring when he went on and on. But Diwali was near, and the air bristled with anticipation and mystery. Mummy had said that Goddess Lakshmi was a very important part of Diwali, and that sometimes she even visited people. Of course, she would only stop at houses that were sparkling clean, and where people were good and their hearts were pure. Mona wondered if the goddess would come to their house this year. Their house was *really clean,* reasoned the little girl. But what about pure hearts? Did puh-TAH'-kay count? She didn't think that puh-TAH'-kay were actually bad, even though forbidden in her own family. But what about the secret? Were secrets bad? Not always. These thoughts were confusing and worrisome, so much so that Mona pushed them aside, and began to dream—to fantasize. *"I will invite Lakshmi,"* she decided. And Mona started to formulate an invitation, a prayer:

"Oh Lakshmi come. We wait for you ..."

What else could she say? She wasn't sure ... so quietly, she joined her brothers as they lowered themselves to the freshly polished floor. They sat cross-legged by Papa's big, soft chair—waiting for tea and for their papa's plan.

Just then, he returned from the kitchen and headed for his chair. His eyes sparkled with excitement. Would he reveal his plan now? Mona held her breath. Sunil squirmed. Mohan sat straight, crossed-legged, and stone-faced. They waited with eyes wide and ears open.

CHAPTER 3

LAKSHMI

"Mmmm," murmured Mona, licking her lips. Ram Lal had just brought a pot of tea from the kitchen. He smiled at her as he leaned down to pour hot liquid into the cup she held toward him. His thin hands, one supporting the spout, the other gripping the handle, carefully tilted the pot as the steaming tea curled downward into her cup. Mona closed her eyes. She loved that sound. It was an invitation to sit and sip. Then she opened her eyes again, and smiled back at the old man who had been with the family for as long as she could remember. "Mummy makes the best tea," she said. He nodded and smiled again, revealing a missing front tooth, as he moved on to pour tea for the others. Sitting quietly, Mona took little sips from her cup. Oh, she liked her tea. It was warm, sweet, and spicy. She watched her papa tilt his cup and take a sip. He slurped a little as he drank, crooking his pinky finger while tipping the delicate cup. After another noisy slurp, Papa cleared his throat.

"We'll go to the market soon," he said. "But first, let's talk about the holiday."

A collective groan greeted that suggestion. Enthusiasm flew out the door. What about Papa's plan? That unspoken question hovered like a cloud over the children. Mona put voice to it. "But Papa, you said you'd tell us about your plan."

"I will," replied her father. "But first, we need to talk about what we do for Diwali and why we celebrate." Another groan—a huge one. Papa raised a knowing eyebrow. "You'll understand my plan better if we do this," he said. "So ... what do we do on Diwali? We'll start with that."

"Well," began Mona, determined to please her father. "Mummy makes special sweets for us and for company. She makes a design on the doorstep too—with rice powder." Mona paused to think about the beautiful *rangoli* design her mum had promised she could help with this year. Lines, spaces, and colors swirled through Mona's head at the very thought of this new, grown-up responsibility.

"I know! I know!" interrupted Sunil with returned enthusiasm. "We have little lights everywhere." Mona smiled because Sunil was remembering their conversation about the lights he would see as they walked to market, and the roof of lights over the road.

"Oh yes," laughed Papa. "There are lights, lots of them. And do you know why?"

"Because it's Diwali," replied Sunil smugly.

"True." Papa paused then, and turned his gaze to Mona. "What do you think, *Bay-tee*? Why do we have lights everywhere, even right up to our door?"

Mona screwed up her brow and responded slowly. "I think it's so Goddess Lakshmi can find us—and come see us. Is that right, Papa?" Mona's hope for a divine visit was increasing.

"Yes, although there's more to Lakshmi than just the lights."

"More?"

"Well . . ." said Papa, measuring his words. "Tomorrow is the first day of Diwali and we do want to please Lakshmi. So it's true that we set out those lights to welcome her. We believe she brings good fortune and even wealth to us and we want that, of course. But she wants something from us too."

"What does she want from us, Papa?" asked Mona anxiously.

"She wants us to welcome her with kind and pure hearts."

"I know that, Papa."

"And, being in charge of wealth and good fortune," he continued, "recognizing and honoring Lakshmi marks the start of a new business year. Did you know that?" Papa didn't wait for an answer, but continued. "That's why I had to work today. I had to close the books for this year and get set up for next year. Everything has to balance honestly and correctly. That is what Lakshmi expects of your papa. Then I could come home and celebrate Diwali with you—with a clear conscience—and help you light the little lamps that welcome her."

Honest and correct? Mona looked at the room around her. Spotless. Spotless is good. It's correct. But what about honest? Her earlier anxiety surfaced. Were secrets honest? Were they pure? *"That depends,"* she thought. Birthday secrets? Gift secrets? Mona decided they were all right. But sneaky secrets that broke rules ...? Suddenly, fear overwhelmed her. Her heart pounded, and she felt sick. Were all these puh-TAH'-kay plans honest and pure? Mona drew into herself, took a deep breath, and called for help. *"Oh, please, Dear Lakshmi, come to our house, please."* Gradually the entreaty settled into a prayer, Mona's very own mantra:

> *"Oh, Lakshmi come. We welcome you.*
> *Our house is clean. Our hearts are pure."*

Mohan had been holding back, but now he took a deep breath, and gazing into his teacup, spoke softly. "Some people shoot Puh-TAH'-kay on Diwali," he said, peering at Papa from hooded eyes. Mona gasped at the cheeky comment. She glanced at Sunil, whose mouth flew open, ready to speak out. So she jabbed him with her elbow.

"Ouch!" he squealed.

Papa grinned. "Puh-TAH'-kay! Oh yes, that definitely is part of my plan. Not all of it, but certainly part of it."

For a shocked moment, no one spoke.

"But we never shoot puh-TAH'-kay!" ventured Mona.

Papa smiled mysteriously. "I know. Fireworks can be dangerous. I found that out years ago." He held out his right hand, palm up, to show a tight scar crossing the palm.

"Oooh Papa," breathed Mona, as she touched the scar lightly. "I never saw that before. What happened? Did it hurt a lot?"

"I've always been careful not to show it to you," said her father. "But it's hard to hide, so I guess it's time for you to see it, especially now ... since shooting puh-TAH'-kay is part of my Diwali plan, as well as the reason for this scar." Papa had the children's full attention now.

"When I was a boy," he began, "Dada and I shot puh-TAH'-kay every year at Diwali. One year, when I was about your age Mohan, Dada gave permission for me to shoot a very special one—a very large one—if I'd be careful. Well, I wasn't careful, and BOOM! It went off in my hand. Then ZOOM! We went off to the hospital. You can imagine that the next explosion came from Dadi when she saw what had happened. No more puh-TAH'-kay! And to this day we haven't argued with her. Ever!"

"But why now?" persisted Mona.

"You're wondering why I would suggest shooting puh-TAH'-kay this year?" Mona nodded. "Because, Bay-tee," Papa said, glancing toward Mohan, "sometime, someone will decide to do it secretly. I know. I was a boy once. Could shooting puh-TAH'-kay be the plan you were trying to tell me about, Sunil?" Sunil's mouth fell open. Mohan gulped. Mona pursed her lips and nodded critically. Papa continued without comment. "I decided that this year we will shoot puh-TAH'-kay together, with supervision, and with attention to safety."

"But what will Mummy say?" asked Mona. "I don't want Mummy to be cross with us." Papa leaned forward and took Mona's face in his hands. He pushed a stray lock from her forehead.

"She knows, Bay-tee. Do you think I would make a decision like that without her consent? At first she objected. But we discussed it and I promised to be careful. I told her, as I've told you, that it's better to shoot puh-TAH'-kay with supervision, knowing in my heart that someday it may be done secretly. Finally, she said okay, but added that she and Dadi will not watch. They'll stay in the house and prepare treats for any friends who stop by. Now! We must be off to market to take care of the next step in my plan—gifts for your mum and for Dadi. We can talk again later, because I want to read an exciting story to you. It's another part of my Diwali plan. You know the story of Rama and Sita, don't you?"

"Well, sure," ventured Mohan. "What about it?"

"You may not have thought much about it," countered Papa. "You're so used to hearing about Rama. But the lights of Diwali are for him and for Sita too."

Mohan didn't look impressed. Neither did Mona nor Sunil, but they said nothing.

"It's a story about duty, and about honoring your word—no matter what. But there's adventure too, Mohan," said Papa. "The lights that welcome Lakshmi also welcomed Rama and Sita when they came home after many dangerous adventures. Their story was told and retold long before it was written down. And even though we have it in written form now, there are many versions."

"But it's boring, Papa. Old people and priests are always talking about Rama. Rama this and Rama that. What's so great about Rama?"

"True, son," smiled Papa. "Old people and priests talk about Rama's story a lot, because it's full of wisdom and examples for living. It's also exciting and there's lots of action. I guarantee you, Rama's story is not boring. However, we have things to do right now. So, *Chul-lo*, my dears! Come on. Let's go to market."

CHAPTER 4

CHUL-LO, TO MARKET WE GO!

"Will Mummy come with us?" asked Sunil, looking back toward the kitchen as he stepped out the front door. Mona knew that Sunil loved to hold his mother's hand when the family went marketing. It made him feel safe and happy. She smiled at him and shook her head.

"Think about it," snapped Mohan. "We're going to buy a kitchen pot for Mum. It's a surprise. It won't be a surprise if she comes with us."

"Oh ..." Sunil's face fell. He moved closer then, to his father. His small hand reached up to Papa, who wordlessly took the outstretched fingers, and squeezed them reassuringly.

"Away we go," said Papa. "Chul-lo, chul-lo." And out the door they went. Papa called to Mum in the kitchen, "We should be back by dark or a little after."

As they trudged down the dirt road, little puffs of dust rose with each step. Mona scrunched her toes into her sandals and looked down to see dust sifting up between them, clouding the shiny red toenails Mum had painted earlier that day.

Neighbors called out as they passed. Mohan waved and saluted one of his friends, who had strings of lights hanging from his shoulders, ready for his papa's command to pass them up. That papa was teetering on a rickety, wooden ladder. The family apparently wasn't lucky enough to have someone like Ram Lal to help them. All along the road, people were stringing lights on courtyard walls, around windows and roofs, just like they did every year. Others were busy placing tiny oil lamps in every possible niche. Diwali was just around the corner. Excitement filled the air.

The little group followed the road, twisting and turning on its way to a central area of the town. Gradually, rows of houses were joined by stalls and low buildings. Mona was in another world, enjoying the lights strung high overhead—the ceiling of lights she had described to Sunil earlier. Popular movie music blared over loudspeakers. Shoppers' voices added to the hubbub, producing a fog of joyful madness. Soon it would be dark. Little by little, lights blinked on around houses and buildings, adding their glow to the lights overhead.

"Are you still with us, Bay-tee?" Mona heard Papa's voice from what seemed like far away. She dragged her thoughts back from the road and the noisy market, and blinked. Papa repeated his question.

"I was just thinking about Goddess Lakshmi, Papa. I want her to come to our house. I really, really do. Oh, please say she'll come. Make her come to see us." Mona's heart throbbed with a growing hope for a visit from the goddess.

Papa's face showed concern over the intensity of Mona's expectations. "She's always welcome and invited, Bay-tee," he said gently. "But I can't order a goddess about. You know that. She's in your heart. You can feel her there."

"Then I'll find her in my coloring book when we get home," finished Mona with a pout. "I'll color her with a beautiful red *sari*, and lots of jewelry. She'll like that. Maybe then she'll come to see us."

Avoiding further comment about a Lakshmi visit, Papa changed the subject. "Remember, Bay-tee, Diwali is about Rama too. The lights we set out are for him and Sita, as well as for Lakshmi. I'll tell you more about that at home—this evening.

Three blank faces turned toward Papa. He tilted his head and suppressed a smile. "You see," he said, "Rama and Sita are the second part of my Diwali plan. First there's Lakshmi's day, and we're on our way right now to buy gifts to honor her day. Then there is the story of Rama and Sita tonight, and finally tomorrow, we'll shoot puh-TAH'-kay!"

"Yay!" cried the children in unison.

Papa slowed his pace. "That will be fun, for sure," he said, resuming his stride. "Tonight, I'll read to you from the book I had as a child. Dada read it to me every year. It's about Rama and Sita, and ... oh, here we are! The first stalls!"

Crowds of celebrants swarmed the lane, milling about, stopping for sweets, shoving, and calling out. Papa told the children to hold hands. No more talk of plans.

Mona was transfixed by the sights and sounds of the holiday melee. She watched a motorcycle rumble by and pop its motor as it slowed and squeezed into an opening at the side of the road. A family of five spilled off the parked two-wheeler, two older children first, then a mother holding an infant. The father, who looked slightly dazed, secured his precious vehicle and joined the others in their shopping adventure. Off to the side of the main road, Mona saw four boys teasing a donkey. It brayed and kicked out. That encouraged further teasing. But the donkey's owner burst out of the crowd, waving a stick and shouting at the boys, who laughed and took off, looking for new mischief.

"Stay close to me," commanded Papa. He looked around until he saw a stall that had kitchen items on display. "Here! Just look at these pots!" Rows of pots and other utensils gleamed under the shop's lights, inviting passersby to stop and look. "I know the owner of this stall," continued Papa. "He's a good man and I trust him, so we'll stop here and look for your mum's new pot."

CHAPTER 5

LOST

Papa stepped forward, his eyes searching the rows of pots on display. "I happen to know that your mum needs a big pot, one like these in the back row. Here's one," he said, releasing his hold on Sunil. He reached over and hefted a large, shiny vessel. "Here ... what do you think of this one?" He turned it this way and that. The children laughed because the pot's shiny, bulging sides reflected Papa's out-of-shape face. They took turns standing near it themselves, making faces, smiling, stepping close, and backing away. They laughed as the image changed: long face, fat face, big eyes, big nose. "All right, all right. That's enough," said Papa. "Is this the right one? Shall we buy this pot for your mum?"

"I'll buy it," interrupted Mohan, drawing the wad of rupees from his pocket.

"That's a lot of money, Mohan," observed Papa. "Did you save up for some kind of grand plan like—oh, maybe to buy some puh-TAH'-kay?" Mohan nodded. "So, I suppose you have matches too?" The twelve year old nodded again, but said nothing.

Papa shook his head and said, "You're a good boy, Mohan, but sometimes you come up with some scary ideas. I suspected that the plan Sunil tried to tell me about had to do with puh-TAH'-kay. Your offer is generous, but it's not fair, Bay-ta. Your mum's pot is from all four of us. So why don't I buy it? We'll have the bottom engraved with all our names—*To Mum from Mohan, Mona, Sunil, and Papa.*" He looked around the group for approval. "How does that sound? You can buy the puh-TAH'-kay, Mohan—with your saved-up pile of rupees. Okay?"

"Yes!" chorused Mona and Sunil. Mohan stood quietly for a moment, then nodded and stuffed his precious money back into a pocket.

"I'd like that," he said.

"But what about a gift for Dadi?" asked Mona, returning to the pot-buying business.

"Umm, yes. What about Dadi?" answered Papa. "Why don't we buy three little spice pots for her? One from each of you. She can keep special spices in them."

Carefully, each child chose a tiny lidded pot. "Mine must say *from Sunil,*" demanded the five year old.

Papa's eyes widened. "Yes, indeed! Each of you should have your name on the little pot that you give to Dadi. Then she will think of you every time she takes spice from it." Papa turned to the merchant and gave all the pots over for the engraving of names.

"But what about your gift, Papa?" continued Mona. "Dadi is your mum. Will you buy Dadi a big pot too?"

"*Dadi* has all the big pots she needs, Mona. I bought a pretty sari for Dadi the other day. Just wait till you see it. It's from me alone— from her own little boy. Do you like that idea?" Mona nodded. Sunil hopped around excitedly. Mohan consented silently and smiled as he patted the bulge of rupees in his pocket.

The merchant gave an assistant the four pots for engraving, then finally placed each tiny spice pot in its own small plastic bag. He reached under his display table for a large bag to hold the large pot for Mum. Papa counted out rupees and paid the merchant. Then he wished the man a happy Diwali, and they started off in search of puh-TAH'-kay.

"Here we go," he announced, then stopped suddenly in his tracks. "Where's Sunil?" Mona's heart leaped. Mohan shrugged his shoulders and began to scan the crowd.

"Sunil!" bellowed Papa. "Follow me, Mona," he said, grabbing her hand. "Mohan, you know the market. Search down around the sari lane and meet us up at the little shrine. It's near some food stalls." Papa and Mona disappeared into the crowd of shoppers. Mohan tore off toward the sari shops.

Still gripping Mona's hand, Papa picked his way through the crowds, looking right and left, calling Sunil's name every few steps. They weren't making any progress. Mona scuffed her new *chup-pals* and stubbed a toe on a rock in the path. She looked down to see that the red polish on the stubbed toe was chipped. But no matter. They had to find Sunil. She could hardly breathe, partly from fear and partly from the breathless pace set by Papa. Breathless too, and discouraged, he finally slowed to a walk. They had reached the little shrine where they planned to meet Mohan. Quietly, they stood next to the shrine and scanned their surroundings. Nothing. No Mohan. No Sunil. Papa clutched Mona's hand so tightly that it hurt, and she was about to say something when she felt a gentle tug at her frock from behind. She whirled, almost twisting away from Papa's grip, only to see that it was Sunil.

"Oh, Sunil, little brother, we thought you were lost."

"I was." He choked back a sob. Huge brown eyes brimmed with tears that made rivers as they spilled out and coursed down his dusty cheeks.

"Why? What?" Mona couldn't think of what to say. She was so relieved, and angry at the same time.

Papa, on the other hand, looked like he had plenty to say. He swallowed hard and worked his jaw, then let loose. "What were you thinking, Sunil? I told you to stay near us, and off you went. Why?" He stopped, took a deep breath, and then bent and scooped Sunil into his arms, hugging the little boy to his broad chest. "Sunil, Sunil, Bay-ta. Why did you run off?" Papa set the little boy back on his feet and stood looking at the dusty runaway.

"I saw Dada up ahead of our stall," gasped Sunil. "I ran after him and called him, but he wouldn't stop. He didn't see me, so I followed him and pulled on his *kurta*." Sunil stopped to catch his breath. "But it wasn't Dada. I didn't know him, and I didn't know where I was. I was so scared, Papa. But I was brave. I did cry a little, but not out loud. I was brave, wasn't I, Papa?" Sunil's whole young body shook with the sobs he'd been holding back. Tears sprang from his eyes like huge rain drops.

Papa relaxed then and smiled. "Yes indeed, Bay-ta. You were brave. You are very brave. But you are not so wise."

Sunil looked puzzled. "Why am I not so wise, Papa?" By this time, his sobs had subsided to rhythmic hiccups. "Am I bad, Papa, because I'm not so wise?"

"*A-ray bop*, child!" exclaimed his father. "That is a hard question. You're not bad, my son. Wise is something else. You are wise when you know the right thing to do—at the right time. You'll learn. It takes a long time." Papa paused then to take a breath before continuing. "Lord Rama had to learn what it means to be wise and to make careful choices. His father, the old king, learned too—but it was too late. His heart was broken because he made a choice without thinking, and that was not wise at all. We'll talk about that later, when we get home ... and I tell you about the adventures of Rama.

"But now we must find Mohan, so we can purchase the puh-TAH'-kay and head for home. Your mum will be looking for us, and it's our duty to come right home from the market—because we said we would."

"Look over there! I see Mohan," cried Mona, pointing. "Mohan! Mohan! Over here. Sunil is here with us."

Mohan's face lit up. He charged through the crowd, then skidded to a stop, panting. "Where were you, Sunil? Where did you go?"

"Never mind that for now, Mohan," said Papa. "We must choose the puh-TAH'-kay quickly, and then hurry home. Come."

CHAPTER 6

AN UNEXPECTED ENCOUNTER

Having made their final purchases, the weary group, arms loaded with bags, shouldered their way through the crowds toward the turn in the road that led home. Papa carried the bag with Mum's large pot in one hand, and clung tightly to Sunil's hand with the other. Mona carried the three little bags with small pots for Dadi, and Mohan bore the precious load of puh-TAH'-kay. Suddenly, Papa stopped. As one, the children jolted to a halt. Mohan crashed into Mona. Mona crashed into Papa, and Sunil staggered to a stop, still clinging desperately to his father's hand.

"Sharma-*ji!*" shouted Papa over the crowds. Ahead, a tall, distinguished-looking man turned to scan the surging mass. When he saw Papa, he waved.

"Hurry up," Papa urged the children. "Mr. Sharma's up ahead. Do you remember him? He was my boss for many years, and now he's retired. His children are grown and he and Mrs. Sharma live in another part of our city. I've not seen him in a long time. Hurry up. You must meet him again."

Elbowing through the crowd, and dragging Sunil along by his hand, Papa carved a path toward his old friend and employer. Mona and Mohan struggled in his wake.

Mr. Sharma and Papa met each other with hands clasped in the *namaste* gesture of greeting (Papa had to drop Sunil's hand and tuck Mum's pot under an arm to do that). "Namaste, Sharma-ji," said Papa, tilting his head respectfully. "What good fortune to meet you this Diwali season!"

"And you also," smiled the older man, returning the namaste.

Stepping aside, Papa indicated his family. "You must remember my children, although they have grown so much, you may not recognize them."

"Indeed, I do remember them, but as you say, they certainly have grown." Sharma's eyes darted from one of the children to another, and then back to Papa. "Speaking of children and changes, my son, Raj, is visiting from America. He's been there now for five years, and was promoted just recently to a new position as a computer consultant for several companies. I'll ask him to stop by your home tomorrow evening. Will you be there?"

Papa wagged his head affirmatively.

"Raj has a surprise," continued Mr. Sharma, and noticing Papa's inquisitive look, said, "no hints though. Just wait and you'll see. It's a good surprise." His eyes twinkled conspiratorially. "May I count on your hospitality?"

"Of course, of course. What a delight! May we look for you and Mrs. Sharma also?"

"Thank you, no. We have guests coming and must be at the house to greet them."

"Very well," smiled Papa. "We'll be home to welcome Raj and his surprise." With smiles and much wagging of heads, the men prepared to take leave of each other. "Are you sure you won't give us a hint about Raj's surprise?" called Papa as they parted.

"*Nahii*, no hints," replied Sharma with a broad smile. "But I must move on. It was so good to see you. Please look for Raj tomorrow evening." Sharma placed his palms together, signaling a namaste fare-well, then hurried off into the crowd.

Mona wondered what that surprise could be, but quickly dismissed the thought. She could just barely remember handsome Raj, but although his visit would be nice, it was not the visit she was hoping for. Raj's visit couldn't in any way compare with that. And Mona softly uttered the prayer, which by now, was clearly her mantra:

"Oh, Lakshmi come. We welcome you.
Our house is clean. Our hearts are pure."

"What did you say, Mona?" asked Papa, turning mid-stride as he guided them through the crowds.

"Nothing," she replied shyly. "I was just thinking out loud."

CHAPTER 7

RAMA,
THE STORY
WITHIN

Mona was pleased with herself. That prayer, her mantra, had popped into her head spontaneously, so it must be powerful. Softly, she repeated it over and over, thinking that by doing this, it would become even more powerful and be heard by the goddess. Surely then, Lakshmi would visit their home. After all, their house was sparkly clean, and having been cleansed of the secret puh-TAH'-kay plans, their hearts were pure too. That's what Mona thought as she murmured her prayer again.

"Oh, Lakshmi come. We welcome you.
Our house is clean. Our hearts are pure."

Papa glanced at his daughter again, but said nothing and plowed on toward home.

When they arrived at the house, the children sped off in three directions, while Papa quietly stowed the gift bags. He seated himself comfortably in his big chair, and in a loud voice, announced, "It's Rama's turn now. Come! Sit!" Each child skidded to a halt and returned to where Papa sat.

"What do you mean, Papa?" asked Mona breathlessly.

"Well, you may recall that I said there's a Rama part to my Diwali plan too. It's very important. So sit down." He gestured toward the floor by his chair. "Here." Papa was holding the old book from his childhood. Its ragged pages showed that it had been much loved over many years. "This is a story of Rama and his wife, Sita."

"We know all about Rama and Sita," exclaimed Mohan. "Do we have to listen to that?"

"Yes, you do," said Papa. "Rama's story is an important part of Diwali. You already know that it tells about good and evil, and about one's true duty. But do you realize that this ancient tale is full of adventure too?"

By this time, the children had squatted to sit cross-legged by Papa's big chair. Mohan folded his arms across his chest mulishly. Mona and Sunil tried to look interested.

Papa ignored their indifference, and launched into a short synopsis. "A young queen had a secret plan. As a result of this plan, an old king died of a broken heart, because once—just once—he made an unwise promise to the young queen. That single mistake changed everything for his son, Rama, for Rama's wife, Sita, and for all the people in the peaceful city of A-yodh-ya."

Papa leaned forward and eyed each child. "A shape-shifting demon lured Rama deep into the forest," he said. "While Sita was alone and unprotected, the king of demons, Ravana, kidnapped her, and carried her away in his magic chariot. A flying monkey found her, and in the end, helped Rama rescue his beloved Sita." Papa sat back in his chair.

"It's a long story," he said. "And this little book doesn't tell every-thing. But it includes many of Rama's adventures, and teaches us what it means to be really wise." Papa glanced over at Sunil, then cleared his throat, ready to begin the story. The children settled into comfortable positions, for truth be known, they loved adventure stories—especially Sunil, who wanted to hear about the flying monkey.

"Did the monkey really fly, Papa?" he asked.

Papa winked at him. "Wait and see, Bay-ta." And he began to read.

> A long time ago, it happened that Rama's father, a good king, who dearly loved his family (particularly his wives) made a foolish promise to his youngest wife—who was exceedingly beautiful and clever. She had plans and approached her husband one day. "Would you please grant me a special favor ... a boon?" she asked, speaking sweetly and lowering her eyes humbly.
>
> "Anything," smiled the king. "Just ask ... anything."
>
> This clever wife touched his feet and backed away, murmuring, "To be sure, I shall remember your promise—always!" Then she left the room with a secret smile on her lips.
>
> The day arrived when the king, who was now more than nine thousand years old—

"Nine thousand years old!" exclaimed Mohan. "That's impossible!"

Papa held up a hand and locked eyes with Mohan. "This is a very old story," he said, "and a powerful one. Who knows how much of it is completely true, and how much is legend ... or if it even matters? It teaches us so much. So please, let me continue."

Mohan lowered his eyes. "*Maaf'-ki'-ji-ay* ... sorry, Papa."

Papa bobbed his head, and returned to the page.

The day arrived when the king, who was now more than nine thousand years old, decided to retire from his throne. He would choose one of his four sons to replace him. The old king chose Rama, the eldest, who was also his favorite.

"Am I your favorite?" chirped Sunil, who by this time, had crawled up to the comfort of Papa's lap.

His father chuckled. "You are all my favorites. How could I possibly choose?"

"The king chose," said Mona righteously.

"Yes, he did. He did have favorites ... not a wise nor loving thing. But I can't finish this story if you keep interrupting me." Papa waited a moment, adjusted his glasses and continued.

The clever queen decided that now was the time to demand the boon her husband had promised her. And that she did. She approached the old ruler, this time boldly. "You promised," she said cunningly, "that I could collect a favor ... anything, any time."

"Indeed I did," smiled the king. "This day of my retirement is a happy one, and important to me too. So I feel most generous. What is your wish, my dear?"

The cunning queen stood upright and proud. "My wish is ... that *my* son, Bharata, sit on the throne, and that Rama leave our city and be banished to the forests of India for fourteen years. That is my wish, oh King, and I know it shall be granted, because you are an honorable man. You will keep your promise."

The king was devastated. The audacity of that young queen! But the truth was, he *had* promised. It was now his duty to keep the promise. However, the king was never the same again, and he died of a broken heart shortly after Rama left the kingdom. For Rama did leave. He understood that it was his duty to obey his father, and he left without complaint. Sita demanded to go with him. She loved her husband deeply and said that she could not live without him. The youngest of Rama's three brothers, Lakshman, chose also to leave with the couple ... to help them, and to protect Sita.

Papa stopped and looked up. "Don't confuse his name with Lakshmi, the goddess. He is Lakshman, the brother." Then he continued.

Many things happened after Rama left beautiful A-yodh-ya, the city of his birth. His brother Bharata declared firmly that he would not sit on the throne in place of Rama. As the eldest son, Rama was the true heir to the throne. Furthermore, Bharata loved Rama and would not, under any circumstances, take his place. So Bharata cleverly placed a pair of Rama's sandals on the throne's silken pillow, thus representing the true king. The sandals would remain there until the fourteen-year banishment should pass. Bharata did, however, take care of the city's day-to-day business from another location near the palace.

Meanwhile, Rama, Sita, and Lakshman roamed the forests of India. They encountered *rishis* (holy men),

who begged Rama to rid the forests of demons, who
had been tormenting them constantly for many years.
At first, Rama refused to confront the demons. He
was a man of peace, he declared, and against any violence. Lakshman chided his brother. "As the eldest of
Father's sons, you are true heir to the throne, and your
kingly duty is to protect these rishis, even if you must
do violence against the demons."

Rama thought hard about this and decided that
Lakshman was correct. It was his duty to rid the forest
of those demons. And so he did. *"Things will be peaceful now,"* he thought. The demons were gone. The
forest was quiet.

Papa looked up at the children. "What do you think? Would the
forest be peaceful now?"

No answer. Silence and three blank stares. "Tell us what happened
next, Papa," urged Mona.

"Very well," said their father, and he turned the page to continue
the story.

Eventually, the three found a place to settle, and
Lakshman built a cozy hut for shelter ... and for
Sita's protection.

Sita loved this life with nature. She spoke softly to the
animals and birds, who felt safe with her and gathered
daily to hear her voice and accept her gentle caresses.
One morning a small, golden deer cavorted near Sita,
who was gathering flowers for her hair. Overcome by

its beauty, she approached the little deer, but it skittered away, ever out of her reach. "Rama!" cried Sita. "Catch this lovely deer for me, and tell it not to be afraid. I only wish to play with it for a while."

Rama tried, but the deer skipped away, slipping like quicksilver, deeper and deeper into the forest. There was no capturing it. "Stop!" commanded Rama.

"Never!" retorted the deer hoarsely. At that moment, Rama realized this was not a deer at all, but a demon, disguised as a deer. So he shot one of his magic arrows and struck the deer. As it fell, it cried out in a voice that sounded exactly like Rama's. "Lakshman! Lakshman! Save me. I need your help."

Sita and Lakshman heard the cries, and Sita commanded her brother-in-law to go and help their beloved Rama. She would be fine in the hut, she declared. Reluctantly, Lakshman set out to find his brother.

"That decision was a disaster," said Papa.
"Why?" cried Sunil. "Did the demon wake up and hurt Rama?"
"No, the demon did not wake up and hurt Rama. The real disaster was happening back at the unguarded hut. Let's see what happens next."

Time passed and Sita began to worry. The brothers had not returned, so she went to the door of the hut ... and there stood a frail old man. He looked so

pathetic that Sita asked if she could help him. Indeed
she could, she was told, if he could only have a cup of
water. Sita's heart was pure. She could not bear to see
suffering, so she fetched a cup of water from within
the hut and brought it to the frail old man.

Papa paused and coughed lightly. "I could use some water myself,"
he said. "Ram Lal! Would you bring me a glass of water please? My
lap is full of Sunil and I'm stuck in this chair."

Hearing Ram Lal's name, Sunil's eyes flew open. "Papa, is Rama
our Ram Lal's grandfather?" he asked. "His name is almost the same."

"I-I don't think so, Sunil," sputtered Papa, holding back a chuckle.
"Rama is very important and famous here in India. Many people
name their children to honor him. They hope that a holy name will
bring their child good fortune.

"Ram Lal," said Papa, accepting a glass of water from his friend
and helper, "you carry a powerful name, and I'd say you're worthy of
it. Don't you think so, children?"

That was a new idea! They'd never thought of Ram Lal as powerful. He was their friend and always around to help them. But powerful? That was something to think about—later.

"Well, back to Sita and the frail old man," said Papa, setting his
water glass on the little table beside his chair. He turned the page and
began to read again.

That frail old man was none other than a disguised
Ravana, the demon ruler, whose island kingdom,
Lanka, was many miles across the sea from India. He
wanted to have Sita for his wife. So he had decided
to kidnap her, and then somehow, get rid of Rama.
Ravana grabbed the frightened Sita and dragged her,

kicking and screaming, to his magic flying chariot, which was hidden among some nearby trees. Off they flew to Lanka, the island kingdom across the sea. Ravana was so pleased with himself that he didn't keep track of Sita, who was sitting behind him in the chariot. She was busily dropping her jewelry along the way, leaving clues, and hoping that the clues would help Rama find her.

Meanwhile, Rama and Lakshman returned to the cottage. No Sita! They were frantic, because they were sure that something bad had happened to her. They began to search for her, all the while calling her name. "Sita! Sita!" There was no answer, of course, for the unlucky Sita was, by this time, plunked into a garden ... held prisoner on the island of Lanka. There, she was guarded by many demon ladies, who didn't particularly like her. So she spent her time lonely and weeping.

"Oh, Papa," interrupted Mona, leaning forward to touch her father. "It's so sad. I don't like this adventure."

"Patience, Bay-tee. Things may change." Papa smiled and picked up the story again.

While the two brothers scoured the forests for Sita, they met a strangely bedraggled monkey. Lakshman urged Rama to ignore it and not waste time getting acquainted with such an unkempt beast. It was just a monkey after all. But Rama could tell that this was no ordinary monkey. Therefore, he greeted him

politely and introduced himself, as was the duty of a
kingly person.

The monkey bowed and touched Rama's feet. "I know
who you are," he said, "but I was not sure you were a
man of honor. That is why I came to you as a beggar
beast." He threw off his rags and stood before them,
huge and muscular. "I need your help," he said, "and
I will help you in return." The monkey leaped about,
showing how powerful and agile he was. "My name
is Hanuman."

"Hanuman! I know Hanuman," exclaimed Mohan.
"He was strong ... super-strong." Mohan made fists and puffed out
his chest.
Sunil perked up too. "Was Hanuman a superhero, Papa?"
"Actually, Hanuman was more than a superhero, Sunil. To Hindus,
Hanuman is a deity, a special god. That's better than a superhero. Let's
see, where was I? Oh yes ... here." He fixed his gaze on the page again.

"Rama," said Hanuman, "I know that you seek your
wife. She has been kidnapped by a demon, and I can
help you look for her."

"Your help will be most welcome," replied Rama.
"But how can I help you, as you suggested?"

"That's easy," said Hanuman. "My king, a kindly
monkey, whose name is Sugriva, has lost his kingdom
to his wicked brother. I happen to know that your
bow and its magic arrows are invincible. Therefore, I

ask you to help my king take back his throne. Then he can reclaim the services of his huge monkey army, and they will help you find Sita. I will join them and help you too."

Lakshman kept nudging Rama to alert his brother to the dangers lurking in this kind of arrangement. Rama ignored him, and agreed to Hanuman's proposition.

It worked. With Rama's help, the monkey king, Sugriva, defeated his wicked brother, and immediately set about organizing monkey troops to start the search for Sita. He divided them into four groups and sent monkey warriors east and west, north and south. They were not to return until they had found Sita, or had word of her whereabouts.

The southbound monkeys made a critical discovery. Across the waters between India and the island of Lanka, they could see Lanka's shimmering palaces. Somehow, they sensed that Sita was there, a prisoner of Lanka's demon king, Ravana. Hanuman, excited by this discovery, and surprised at the extent of his own physical powers, leaped across that expanse of waters to look for Sita.

"What?!" cried Mohan. "You can't leap across a sea."
"What did I tell you?" reminded Papa. "This story is legend, mixed up with history. It was told from generation to generation before it was ever written down. There is wisdom in the story and that's why it's important."

"Oh," said Mohan softly.

Papa, as well as the children, was getting restless. He flipped through the remaining pages. "Let's see ... I think I can skip some of these details," he mumbled. The trip to the market and the search for Sunil had been tiring for all of them. "Yes, I'll pick it up here," he said softly. Then he took a deep breath, and plodded on.

> Eventually, Hanuman found Sita, and offered to take her to Rama. But she refused, saying that it was Rama's duty to make the rescue himself. So, dejectedly, Hanuman returned to India and reported everything to Rama, including Sita's challenge.

Papa stopped, lifted his glasses, and rubbed his eyes.

"Well, what happened next?" demanded Mona, still worried about Sita and those unfriendly demon ladies.

Papa smiled wearily, and returned to the story.

> Rama accepted the challenge to perform his duty and rescue Sita himself. Sugriva, the monkey king, declared that his army would assist Rama in this dangerous task. But there had to be a way to reach the far shores of Lanka. A bridge must be built, he declared, and Sugriva set his monkeys to work. They piled stone upon stone, rock on top of rock, until they had built a bridge across the sea, all the way to the island of Lanka.

"How could they do that?" asked Mohan critically.

Papa's tired look changed to one of determination. "You are Indian, my son. This epic—for it is India's great epic—about honor and duty, about how to live as an Indian and a human being, is one to take seriously. Someday you'll know the whole long story. So be proud, Bay-ta, and learn it well." Papa closed his eyes momentarily. "We're getting to the end," he said.

"Oh, all right. But I still think the rocks would sink."

Without further comment, Papa began to read again.

> When Rama and the monkey army completed the crossing and entered Lanka, a fierce and bloody battle ensued. Fallen demons and monkeys carpeted the entire island. In the end, Rama, with his magic bow and arrow, shot and killed Ravana. It was time to go home. The fourteen years of exile were up. So Rama, Sita, and Hanuman piled into Ravana's magic chariot, and flew off, heading for A-yodh-ya and home.

Papa started to close the book.

"Is that it?" asked Mona. "What happened when they got there? There has to be more."

Papa looked at her and said, "Oh yes, Bay-tee, there is always more. Depending on the story-teller, this story continues to grow and change. It has even more characters, and over the ages, has evolved into many versions. But the important themes are always there. Rama, like Lakshmi, shows us how to live good, honorable lives." Papa fingered the last ragged page of the book, turned it, and read the conclusion to this youthful version of Rama's adventures.

> As the chariot circled A-yodh-ya, descending with each pass, bright little lamps and shimmering stars escorted the travelers to their landing. The citizens of A-yodh-ya cheered and danced. They waved and

shouted. They filled the streets, decorated their homes and buildings with lights and more lights. Even elephants, colorfully draped and painted, joined the melee, trumpeting madly. Celebration and lights welcomed their king as he returned to A-yodh-ya and to his people. This dramatic event became part of our Diwali celebration.

"There you have it, my children! Duty and honor. Rama had his own special duties as a ruler and a husband. Hanuman's duty was to his king, Sugriva, and to his friend, Rama. My duty is to you, my darlings, to our family, and to my work." Papa looked at Sunil. "When you understand *your* duty, my son, then you will be wise."

Mona observed Sunil's look, wide-eyed and thoughtful. He opened his mouth as if to say something, and then closed it, turned suddenly, and hugged his papa. "I will be wise, Papa! I know I will. Then, will you call *me* Rama?"

Papa threw back his head and laughed. "Oh no, precious Bay-ta. You will always be Sunil ... my own dear Sunil, and no other."

CHAPTER 8

DIWALI
MORNING

Mona's eyes popped open. Morning. Diwali! All the events of the pre-
vious day whirled through her mind: Lakshmi, Rama, Sita, and the
market. And now, this morning, the rangoli design with Mummy. So
much to do.

Sunlight had crept into the room and brushed night's darkness
into dusty-looking corners. Pulling her mind into the new day, Mona
reasoned that her room couldn't possibly be dusty. She and Mummy
had cleaned and polished, polished and cleaned, for the past few days.
"But that's not important," she thought. *"It's Diwali today!"* And in her
heart, Mona sang a welcoming prayer, a new mantra, to her friend,
the goddess Lakshmi:

> *"Come Lakshmi. It's Diwali day.*
> *Our little lights will show the way."*

Mona giggled at the changed mantra as she threw off the bed
sheet and swung her bare feet to the cool floor. She exchanged her
night clothes for a faded frock, which she would wear until later in
the day when chores were done. Mummy was already at it, humming
and moving about in the outer room. Mona could hardly wait to help

her mother with the beautiful rangoli design at the doorway. But first, there was Mohan. He didn't need to think he'd get by without taking part in their holiday chores.

Mona padded down the short hall to the room where her brothers were sleeping. *"I'm so lucky,"* she thought, *"to have a room all to myself."* Her tiny abode housed a narrow bed, a little table for her books, and a corner niche for her prayer articles. Those rested near pictures of favorite deities, which she had taped to the wall. There was also a metal chest placed beneath a small window. She kept her modest wardrobe in that chest—everything folded neatly.

"Mohan," she half-whispered, poking her head into the boys' room. "Mohan, time to get up. It's Diwali!"

"Mmmph!" Mohan turned over and pulled the bed sheet over his head. One foot was sticking out from under the sheet. Mona tiptoed into the room, grabbed Mohan's big toe, and twisted it.

"Yeow!" Mohan sat up suddenly. "Something just bit me!"

"Nothing bit you, Mohan. You were dreaming. It was me. I grabbed your toe. It's Diwali and it's time to get up. We have to help Mummy and Ram Lal with the work."

Mohan flopped back to hide again beneath his bed sheet.

"Get up or I'll twist your toe again, and I'll tell Mummy you're just a big lazy bones. And be quiet about it or you'll wake Sunil. He'll just pester us."

The two siblings looked over at their younger brother, who lay sprawled on his back, snoring softly.

"Okay, okay. I'm up. Just leave me alone so I can get dressed."

Mona backed out the door and turned her steps toward the outer room. There she could hear Mummy working near the front doorway—humming softly. She was busy with the rangoli design. "Mummy!" cried Mona. "You promised I could help."

"And you shall, Bay-tee. I just finished outlining the design with fine, white rice powder." Mummy stood up and smoothed her sari. "You are so good with colors that your assignment is to fill in the open spaces with these colored powders." Mummy pointed to several little cups near the floral design. Each cup contained a brightly colored powder. "Just be careful not to smear them. And stay inside the lines," she smiled. "When you're finished, I have some more things for you to do. But first, you must eat something. No breakfast this morning. I set out a light snack, with some dates and left over *chap-patis* from yesterday. There's a dish of yogurt too, and a pot of tea. It should still be hot. You can snack all morning between jobs. Later, when Dada and Dadi get here, we'll have a proper dinner. This year we'll be celebrating at our house."

Mona nibbled on a chap-pati—that ever-present Indian flat bread—and sipped some tea. Then she went to the front doorway, knelt, and focused fiercely on the rangoli design. Mummy had outlined a beautiful lotus flower, and surrounded it with leaves and other forms. It did, indeed, need some color; it must be beautiful for Lakshmi. Mona picked up one of the tiny tin funnels Mummy had left for her. Let's see, she thought. Rosy-red first. With a small tool, she spooned rose-colored powder into the funnel and began to work. Oh yes, this would please the goddess. Rosy-red like Lakshmi's sari, then green for leaves. Peacock blue, and yellow designs to surround and set off the central lotus. *"She'll like this,"* thought Mona, and whispered her new mantra as she stood up to admire her work. She smiled to herself, slipped on her old chap-pals, and moved into the courtyard. There, she selected several small rocks, made a pouch for them with the skirt of her frock, and returned to the design in the doorway. Carefully, Mona placed a row of little rocks on each of the four sides of the rangoli design, spacing them like a barrier.

Mummy came from the kitchen to investigate the artist's progress. "Oh!" she exclaimed. "You really are an artist, Mona. You made my simple outline come to life. If you practice, I may even ask you to do the entire design next year." Mummy stood looking at the completed rangoli. Slowly, her forehead puckered into a small frown. "But why are those little rocks at the sides of our design?" she asked.

"It's so no one will step on it, not until Lakshmi sees it. Remember, last year Sunil messed it all up."

Mummy tried to hide her amusement. "That's right, he did," she said. "The rangoli must be protected until Lakshmi comes ... *if she comes*," Mummy finished under her breath.

"She'll come!" retorted the young artist.

"Come Lakshmi. It's Diwali day.
Our little lights will show the way."

CHAPTER 9

IN THE
COURTYARD

Mohan shuffled into the room—barefoot, hair disheveled and stand-ing on end. Mum and Mona gazed at him with raised eyebrows.

He looked at them. "What?"

"You look like someone just dragged you out of a ditch by your hair," giggled Mona.

"I feel like it," said her brother, slumping into a chair.

"There's a snack in the kitchen," said Mum, ignoring the exchange. "You need to eat something before I give you your assignment."

"My assignment?"

"Your Diwali job is quite easy," she continued, "and only a strong young man such as yourself can do it."

"Mummy's a real diplomat," thought Mona. *"I wonder if she really meant it when she called me an artist. But she must have, because I'm really good."*

"Now," stated Mum, as Mohan munched on a dry chap-pati, "come over here. I'd like you to take these sacks of waste papers up to the roof. It's flat up there, so no one will see them from down here if you don't stack them any higher than the half wall. We can dispose of them properly another day. And if Lakshmi comes," she winked at Mona, "I'm sure she won't go up to the roof." The wink made Mona uneasy. She took it to mean that Mum didn't really believe there'd be a Lakshmi visit at all.

Mohan swallowed his last bite and sidled over to his mother. "But Mum," he objected, "why should I do all the hard work?"

Mum stood up straight, hands on her hips. "Hard work, Son? You don't know what hard work is. Ram Lal, out there in the courtyard," she tilted her head toward the doorway, "is preparing our oil lamps. He went to market early this morning and lugged back 150 little clay lamps, as well as the cotton to cut and twist into wicks. He's doing that right now." Mohan cast a wary eye toward the courtyard where Ram Lal was diligently twisting short strips of cotton, obviously ignoring the discussion. Mum persisted. "I've been cleaning and cooking. Mona just finished coloring the rangoli. She'll take a break, and then she'll help me set out the lamps." Having said that, Mum pointed Mohan to the bags of paper near the door and huffed back to Mona to describe her new task.

"Well, what about Papa?" Mohan wasn't ready to quit. "What's Papa going to do?"

Mum's diplomacy vanished. "Your father had to go to work this morning. He left early so he could stop by the market to pick up some last-minute things. He'll be home shortly. You can take up your grievances with him then, if you wish. In the meantime, get yourself over here and take those papers up to the roof!"

"Whoops!" thought Mona. *"Mohan better watch out."* It was well known that Mum seldom lost her temper, but when she did ...

Grumbling, Mohan grabbed two sacks of paper, one in each arm, and clumped up the cement steps that hugged the outside wall of the house. He stomped back down a moment later. Up and down. Up and down ... all the time grumbling. When he had finished with the last bag, he stood back to see if any showed over the half wall surrounding the roof. Nope! All clear. With his lower lip shoved out stubbornly,

Mohan muttered something about lugging paper bags around, which was not part of his duty as the elder son of the family.

Mum ignored him and turned back to Mona. "Come over here with me," she said. "I'll show you what we must do with these little lamps." She walked over to a long table that was set up near the great tree in the courtyard. Ram Lal had just completed preparing the wicks and was filling the lamps with measured amounts of vegetable oil. "See, Bay-tee. Now we must place them carefully along the window-sills, around the door ledges, and on the compound walls. Papa will light them later."

"But I can't reach all those places," whimpered Mona.

"You can reach a lot of them, Bay-tee. Here, I'll show you."

Mona padded reluctantly over to the table to stand by her mother. Dozens of little clay lamps were lined up like tiny soldiers on review. She glanced past the lamps to the rangoli design on the doorstep. It was beautiful, and she had enjoyed filling it with colors. But placing dozens of little oil-filled lamps seemed like a real chore, and Mona began to feel some of Mohan's resentment.

"Here." Mum placed a lamp carefully on a windowsill. "Like this. You see? It takes special care and patience to keep the oil from spilling. Place several little lamps, side by side, everywhere. You have the gift of patience, Bay-tee. You can do it."

"Ah," thought Mona, "Mummy's still a diplomat." They worked together in silence until most of the lamps were in place. Mum took the hard-to-reach ones. Soon, voices floated into the compound from nearby. The iron gate creaked open and in walked Dada, Dadi, and Papa! Mona's pride of accomplishment returned. "Look! See what we've just done!"

"Wonderful!" exclaimed Papa. "I can see you've all been busy."

Mohan, the pride-wounded male, took the opportunity presented by newcomers to rush forward, kneel, and humbly touch first Dada's feet, and then Dadi's.

"Ah," exclaimed Dada, turning to Papa, "a traditional Hindu boy. You've raised him well, my son."

Papa looked a little sheepish. "Well, I ..." He started to protest, and then changed the subject abruptly. "Where is Sunil? Don't tell me we've lost him again." He chuckled to indicate that he was just teasing. "Where is that young one?"

At that moment, Sunil rushed from the house, jumping neatly over the beautiful rangoli. Mona breathed a sigh of relief.

"Dada, Dadi! It's Diwali!" cried the youngster. When he reached his grandfather, Sunil lunged, ending up hugging the old man's legs. Dada staggered back at the impact, but Mona observed that this show of enthusiasm had pleased him just as much as Mohan's traditional greeting.

"It's time for tea," said Mum, wiping her hands on a towel. "I'll go prepare a tray of tea and sweets. Come on in. Sit and rest before we change from our work clothes and get ready for the evening."

CHAPTER 10

GIFTS
AND
PUJA

Papa set his empty teacup on the little stand by his chair. He wiped his lips with the back of his hand and cleared his throat. "Ved Uncle and Mina Auntie won't be joining us for celebration this evening," he said. "Uncle is ill and Auntie will stay with him to observe Diwali at home." After a moment of silence, he turned to Mona and directed her to fetch Dadi and Mum. "Please ask them to come here," he smiled. "It's time for us to share some gifts."

"But Papa, I thought we would do the *puja* ceremony first."

"Normally we would, Bay-tee, but I have a good reason to reverse the order. Now scoot. Go get your Mum and mine." As Mona retreated to the kitchen, where the two women were readying things for a late dinner, Papa called after her. "Have them ask Ram Lal to join us too!"

The two brothers were sitting on the floor near Papa when Mona rejoined them. They were more than ready for gifts—for Dadi, for Mum, and for themselves too, of course. Sunil wriggled with anticipation. Mohan sat stoically. Mona took in a huge breath and exhaled slowly. *"So much more fun to have gift-giving first!"* she thought. *"Puja can wait."*

She knew that for Puja, Dada would act as *pujari*, the priest. He would bathe and feed a small image, then murmur a prayer in Sanskrit (an ancient formal language). Mona was sure it was okay. Lakshmi would understand the changed order of things.

As the family assembled, Papa pulled plastic bags from behind his chair. Mona recognized the ones holding their pots, the ones they had bought in the market the day before. But there were other bags. This didn't surprise her. She knew there would be more gifts. There always were.

The first bag, round and hard, went to Mum. "For me?" she asked, pretending to be surprised. The children beamed as she folded back the plastic to reveal a large pot. She pulled it out of the bag. "Oh, I love it!" she exclaimed. She turned the pot this way and that. She looked at the gleaming surface, and at the distorted, smiling face that looked back at her from its rounded sides. She turned it over, and on the bottom, she could see some scratchings. "I see your names," she said, "all of them. It is just what I needed, and it is so beautiful. I will think of each of you every time I use this pot." Mum cradled it in her arms as she scanned the faces of her family.

Papa beckoned then to his children, and gave each of them a little bag that contained their gifts for Dadi, who accepted them one at a time, until she had collected all three bags. Then she set them on the table by Papa's chair. "*Tink*," said the first bag, as she set it down. "*Tink, tink,*" said the other two, as she placed them on the table near the first.

"What could these be?" wondered Dadi, eyes twinkling. They widened as she felt the bags carefully. "Something inside each bag is round and hard ... and so very little. Shall I look inside?"

"Yes!" cried Sunil. "Look inside this bag." He grabbed one. "It's for you, Dadi."

"*A-ccha'*, good!" Dadi peeked into Sunil's little bag. Something in there glittered. "Why, it's a tiny pot," cried Dadi. She turned it over. "And it says Sunil on the bottom!" She looked up to see the five year old jumping about, clasping his palms excitedly. "I think I'll open the others too," she said. "Ah! This one is from Mona, and I'll just bet the other is from Mohan. I love them all, and they will look so pretty on a shelf in my kitchen. They're perfect for my favorite spices." She turned and showed Dada, who smiled absently.

Poor Dada, thought Mona. All these gifts, but not one for him.

Papa was on a roll. He handed Dadi a soft, flat package next. It was surely not a pot. "Something more for me?" Dadi turned the package over. It was floppy.

Sunil couldn't sit still. "Dadi, it's a—"

"Hush!" Papa put a finger to Sunil's lips.

Carefully, Dadi untied the string and opened the package. Something inside glinted at her, but it wasn't shaped like a pot. Oh no! It turned out to be a sari … a silk, creamy-colored sari with pure gold threads woven into patterns at one end. "Ooh," she said softly. "It's wonderful." She held the sari to her cheek, eyes speaking a silent thanks to her son—her own bay-ta. "I'm so happy for my pots and my sari."

Papa looked proud. "I'm glad you like it, Mum. But I have more." He pulled another flat package from the niche behind his chair and addressed his children. "This one is for your Mum," he said. "I bought it last week—all by myself."

Mum put a hand to her lips to cover a small squeak. Papa handed the package to her. She opened it to find another sari, this one was a bright peacock blue. It too had gold threads woven across one end, but not as much gold as Dadi's. Everyone knew that was appropriate. "It's fantastic," purred Mum. "Just fantastic. And you," she added, nodding to her spouse, "you are a fantastic husband and papa."

Again and again, Papa reached behind his chair. There was a huge book—for Dada—a Hindi version of the *Ramayana,* the Rama story … the whole *long* story! Immediately, Dada began flipping through the pages, stopping at this page and that to exclaim. It was well known that Dada loved the story of Rama, but had never owned a full-sized, illustrated copy of the treasured epic.

Mona smiled at this surprising gift for her grandfather.

Papa kept rolling along. The boys came first. Sunil got a ten-inch figure of Spider-Man in full dress. A brand new cricket bat appeared for Mohan. How had Papa been able to keep that out of sight? Then, came Mona, who by this time, was tense with anticipation. Her eyes told Papa of her curiosity.

"Oh, let's see," he mused. "I think I had something special for Mona too. Now, where could I have put that?" Mona held her breath—hands clasped, her shoulders tightly hunched. "Oh, here it is! It was hiding behind the bookcase." Papa bent to produce a beautiful miniature carving of Lakshmi! She was clothed in a rosy-red sari, and seated on a lotus blossom with her feet tucked into the petals of the flower.

"Oooh," breathed Mona, as she reached for the little figure. She took it carefully and placed it in a cupped palm. Her fingers curled gently about it. "It's perfect. I will set it in my room, on my little puja table. But Papa … I've never thought about it. Why does Lakshmi have so many arms?"

Papa chuckled. "Lakshmi has great powers. Her several arms tell us that. She doesn't have big muscles like Hanuman, does she?" Mona shook her head. "Well, her arms tell the story," said Papa. "It takes a lot of arms to do a lot of things."

All this time, Ram Lal had been standing in the kitchen doorway, quietly watching the gift exchange. A soft smile dominated his age-creased face. Papa got up from his chair and walked over to Ram Lal.

He held out a fat envelope. "Ram Lal, this is for you. You've been with our family for so many years, just like a beloved uncle."

Everyone in the room knew that the envelope contained rupees. They were for Ram Lal to use in any way he liked. The old man placed his palms together, then reached down to touch Papa's feet with his fingertips. He was old-fashioned, and this gesture was his way of expressing his thanks, and how much he loved Papa and the whole family. Mona noticed Dada's fleeting smile, and slight nod. Dada was old-fashioned too, and he understood just what Ram Lal was saying. He was saying much more than thank you. He was wholly pledging his love to Papa and to the family.

"Time for puja now," said Papa abruptly. "Mona, may we use your little Lakshmi on the puja table? Tiny as it is, she looks just like the goddess, and that will help us send our prayers to her. Come. Mum and Dadi have set a puja table over there against the wall." Mona glanced toward the puja table and saw the perfect place to set her little image—in a nest of marigolds and leaves. Her hopes for a visit from Lakshmi were huge by now—and growing. She breathed the words:

"Come Lakshmi. It's Diwali day.
Our little lights will show the way."

CHAPTER 11

DINNER

Prayers were over. Dada had performed the worship ritual carefully and lovingly. He had rung the little brass bell to call the goddess. He had bathed her tiny image by sprinkling drops of milk from his fingertips, and had then symbolically fed her with bits of sweets. Then he turned and placed a small sweet (the *pra-saad)* into each open hand. This done, Dada smiled and looked toward Mum and Dadi. "Time for dinner."

Now it was Mum's turn. Dinner was her specialty. "This holiday meal will be special," she said, "but not huge because we may have visitors before long. Also Dadi and I prefer to have the puh-TAH'-kay explosions cleared off when guests arrive!" She finished the sentence with emphasis and a tiny scowl. Everyone got the message.

While Mum spoke, Dadi rushed to the kitchen to begin assembling the serving dishes. It was usual for Dadi and Mum, together with Mina Auntie, to prepare and serve festival meals each year. They knew exactly what to do, and they did it year after year. But this time, with Ved Uncle's sudden illness, Mum had taken full charge. She'd prepared most of the meal. She'd set her beautiful new table with gleaming stainless steel plates and tumblers—and no cutlery.

"We eat with fingers tonight," mused Mona happily, *"but we don't have to sit on the floor."* She knew that sitting on the floor around a pretty

cloth, and eating with fingers, was Dada's preferred way to share a festive meal. Many times he had declared, "We're Indians. That's how we eat." But Mum was eager this year to serve from her beautiful new mahogany dining table, and so they had compromised. They would eat at the table to please Mum, and with fingers to please Dada. Mona liked that. Sitting at table, and dangling her feet from her chair, made her feel very sophisticated. And Dada didn't fuss at all about table-eating today, because after many years of compliance, he was finally going to shoot off puh-TAH'-kay! That was certainly worth a compromise.

"Sit!" said Mum, unceremoniously. They sat. Even Dadi. She had done her part by helping to serve the food Mum had prepared. The first course of this so-called simple meal featured a platter of steaming vegetable fritters, plus a plate piled high with triangular pastry packets, all stuffed with diced potatoes, peas, and spices. Following these appetizers were rice and lentil curry, spinach with cheese chunks, and chap-patis. A rice and vegetable dish came separately, mounded on an oval platter and garnished with twigs of cilantro. Tiny stainless steel cups ringed the main serving dishes. They contained tomato chutney, mango pickles, and yogurt with diced cucumbers. A huge bowl of plums and grapes completed the meal.

"Yum!" murmured Mona softly.

It was everyone for themselves as they filled their plates and tucked into the food. Mona tried to put thoughts of Lakshmi out of her mind and concentrate completely on the feast. It didn't work. The beautiful goddess danced in and out of her thoughts as she grabbed a chap-pati, pulled a chunk from it, and swept several food choices into the bite-sized packets. She was careful not to let the juice drip down her arms to her elbows. Glancing over at Sunil, Mona smiled to see that he was happily covering his face and clothes with the juice that escaped from his chap-pati packets.

Having eaten her fill, Mona wiped her lips with the back of her hand before she noticed that Mum had placed a small bowl of water near each plate. She dipped her fingers into the water and was about to wipe them on her frock when she noticed a small towel passing from one person to another. Frock saved!

Papa and Dada each produced a healthy burp, entirely acceptable after a meal in India—actually considered a sign that the meal had been appreciated. Mohan attempted a manly burp of his own. Sunil didn't bother. He licked his fingers and helped himself to another chap-pati.

Father and Grandfather were noticeably restless. Dada stood and politely burped again. Papa stood too, shoved his chair to the table, and spoke loudly to Dada—so loudly that any person passing by on the road could have heard him. "It's puh-TAH'-kay time," he announced with a grin. Everything in the room changed. Up popped the children. Mohan arose with such vigor that his chair tipped over backward. Dadi stood and quietly began gathering dishes. Ram Lal sprang into action, assisting her but casting longing looks toward the door to the courtyard. Mum was already in the kitchen, clattering noisily. Mona grabbed her tiny Lakshmi image from its place on the puja table and held it to her breast.

Now for the fun!

CHAPTER 12

POP!
CRACKLE!
FIRE!

Pop! Crack! Fizz! Puh-TAH'-kay!

Papa and Dada were having as much fun as the children. The court-yard was filled with pops, cracks, and tiny colorful explosions. Back in the house, in the kitchen, Mum and Dadi pretended they couldn't hear the commotion. But Mona knew that they heard. The noise was so ... well ... noisy. Mona caught a glimpse of Sunil peeking cautiously from the doorway into the courtyard. Ram Lal stood beside the lad, a hand on his shoulder. The noisy, happy clamor, punctuated by small explosions, welcomed the beginning of Diwali.

Mona's feelings were enormous. She was excited by the beautiful fireworks. She loved to see her father and her grandfather having so much fun. And most importantly, Mona had a nagging hope that Goddess Lakshmi would see their joy, the beauty of their lights, their good humor, and be compelled to stop at their house to share the fun. She didn't know *how* the goddess would appear or *when*. She just hoped with all her heart that she *would* appear. Somehow.

Papa had suggested using Mohan's matches to light the fireworks, and Mohan gladly handed the box to his father, relieved of the guilty feelings he still had about the earlier puh-TAH'-kay plot. Mona was certain of that, because she saw Mohan straighten up and square his shoulders during the transfer.

What fun! Mona's joy danced all around the edges of her continued hope for a divine visit. Her mind constantly swirled with pictures of a smiling Lakshmi standing beside her in the courtyard:

> *"Lakshmi, did you like that little cracker? Oh, Lakshmi, see the puh-TAH'-kay flower that just flew over the house! Aren't you glad you came, Lakshmi? See my beautiful red toes? Even though the polish on my big toe is chipped, it's still beautiful! Oh see, Lakshmi! Please come! You are so welcome!"*

Mona's mind was filled with thoughts of the goddess. She even described, to the divine image in her mind, how very strange the puh-TAH'-kay shapes looked before they exploded. Most were covered in cheap brown paper. One little round, flat one looked like a small mud cake. But when Papa lit the wick with Mohan's match, it uncurled and wiggled and grew to look like a tiny snake or a large worm.

> *"See, Lakshmi. Look at that little snake. It wiggles like it's alive."*

There were tiny firecrackers too, many of them strung together. When Dada lit one, it popped, sending the others pop, pop, popping, until they were all gone. Still others made sparks of many colors. The courtyard was filled with light and noise, and Mona shared every bit of it with her fantasy guest.

Suddenly, Dada lit a high-flyer. *Zoom* it went ... spitting sparks as it climbed up, up, and up. It arced and descended, landing high in the great tree by the wall. Three bright green parrots burst, squawking, from the treetop. That was when Mum and Dadi appeared in the doorway of the house.

Papa looked up. "Good!" he called to his wife. "I was just going to call you. It's time for the last of the fireworks, and we saved the most beautiful one for you, Mum. Come out here. I have something important for you to do."

"We'll be using the last of Mohan's matches too," put in Dada.

"What?" Mum was shocked. "What do you mean, 'Mohan's matches'? And why were those birds squawking out here?"

"I'll tell you about the matches later," said Papa. "But right now, we have one cracker left, the biggest, and most special of them all. And I've decided that you should have the honor of launching it."

"Me?"

"Yes, I'll move over a bit—away from the tree. That last one frightened some birds. Please Mum, the children would love to have you be a part of this. We'd be honored if you'd set off the final flyer."

"Please, please!" chorused Mona and Mohan. Quietly, Sunil slipped out of the front door, to stand silently by Mona in the courtyard—his eyes like saucers.

"Humph!" said Mum.

"Come on," coaxed Papa. "Here, I'll stand right beside you. See? It's safe. I have a bucket of water right here. This cracker will go sky high and it will be fantastic! Then we'll clean up the yard, so that when our guests arrive there won't be a scrap of puh-TAH'-kay left to tell the tale."

Reluctantly, Mum walked slowly toward Papa. She held out her hand for the dreaded match, at the same time glancing toward Mohan. Then she bent to light the last of the puh-TAH'-kay. Dadi stood near the doorway, scowling slightly, her arms folded across her bosom. Mum lit the match, lit the wick of the firework, and ... *PHOOM!*

It streaked toward the stars.

"Oooh!" exclaimed the children.

"Aaah!" uttered Papa and Dada.

Mum and Dadi stood silently, eyes following the trail of light. Then it arced, as did the firework before it, and began to descend. This one headed straight for the house, eliciting a collective gasp from those in the courtyard!

Thud! The still-flaming firework landed on the roof. Immediately, something up there caught fire. Flames leaped high into the sky and began to spread across the roof.

"What! What's that?" shouted Papa. Grabbing his bucket of water, he raced toward the steps that led up to the roof.

"It's the paper," moaned Mum. "I had Mohan take waste papers to the roof this morning." She followed Papa and started up the steps behind him. "It's my fault! It's my fault!" she wailed. I should have said, 'No! No puh-TAH'-kay!'"

Everyone scattered. Mona scooted to the corner of the yard, next to the great tree and hugged herself. Sunil followed and pressed close to his sister. Mohan stood frozen, looking toward the roof. Dada and Dadi clutched each other, eyes wide. Then Dada began to sway to one side as Dadi clung to him.

From the stairs, Papa shouted, "More water! Hurry!"

CHAPTER 13

THINGS SETTLE

Mum stood frozen halfway up the stairs. Black flakes of burnt paper blew all around the roof area and fluttered to the ground, disturbing the tree birds again. Papa and Ram Lal were the only figures in motion, the latter passing more water buckets to Mum, who finally joined the rhythm and passed them on up to Papa, one at a time. Mona had often wondered why there were so many buckets stacked up in their washroom. She still wasn't sure, but for now she was glad for them and gave it no further thought.

Images of Lakshmi rushed through her mind and Mona was crushed. Her wonderful fantasy conversation with the goddess vanished. *Poof!* Where was Lakshmi now? Certainly she was not beside Mona. Had Lakshmi seen the fire, the blackened flakes of paper fluttering all around the courtyard? Surely she had turned away from the mess, gone to other homes that sparkled with clean rooms and welcoming lights. *"After all my prayers,"* grieved Mona. The promises of cleanliness and purity now seemed to be nothing but foolishness. Mona turned all her thoughts inward in utter misery.

Shortly, Papa got the flames under control, but the scene was a disaster. It looked like the whole house had been torched. Debris from fireworks littered the courtyard and the fire itself contributed blackened streaks down the side of the house. There was soot and ash all over. Papa, discouraged, but having drowned the fire, climbed down the stairs slowly, disheveled and looking puzzled. His sweaty face told the story of the battle, and his streaked and wrinkled shirt hung limply outside his trousers. Mona sank sobbing to a sitting position on the doorstep, beside the rangoli design. She reached over and gently touched Lakshmi's beautiful lotus with a fingertip.

"Mona, Bay-tee, the fire is out and no one was hurt," said Mum, bravely trying to hide her own dismay. Nevertheless, she looked pretty sad herself—and angry. "No more!" she spat out, turning to face Papa.

"No more what?"

"No more puh-TAH'-kay!"

"No more of the big ones," countered Papa wearily.

"No more puh-TAH'-kay at all!" Mum set her jaw stubbornly. "It was my fault. I know I should not have asked Mohan to take all those papers to the roof. And it was my fault for agreeing to this fiasco." Mum's voice trembled, and tears spilled down her cheeks.

"It was no one's fault and it was everyone's fault. We all had a hand in this," soothed Papa.

"Not me. What did I do?" quavered Mona. This was more than she could bear. "Sunil didn't do anything either."

"True," said their father. "But we all enjoyed it, and it was fun until that big one caused this problem. The small ones are safe. No problems with them. It's the large ones that get out of hand. I should have known that." He glanced at his scarred palm. "No more big ones for sure! Can you agree to that?" He looked over at Mum.

"No more puh-TAH'-kay," she muttered between clenched teeth.

"By the way," said Papa, changing the subject, "why did you want all that paper on the roof anyway?"

"There wasn't time to dispose of it properly. I was going to see to it after the holiday. But now ... that too, was my fault." And Mum began to sob again, along with Mona—a soppy, sobbing duo.

"Lakshmi won't come to our house now," whispered Mona, her anxiety doubled by Mum's tears.

For a moment, Papa said nothing. He was shaken by the two weeping females and yet another female—his own mum—standing by and scowling. Pulling his thoughts together, he said, "I'll go wash up now and change my clothes." Then starting toward the front door, he stopped short. It wasn't until he had spoken, and looked toward his parents, that he saw his father seated on a rock, slumped, and leaning against Dadi's leg. Papa understood then ... that what seemed at first to be Dadi's anger, was actually fear for her spouse.

"He passed out," she quavered, her hand on Dada's shoulder, while trying to keep her balance against his leaning weight. Dada's face was ashen. He seemed to be folded into himself, unaware of the chaos around him.

Papa looked furtively around until he caught sight of Ram Lal, who had rushed to collect two large cushions from within the house, and was now gently shifting Dada onto them. "Someone fetch some cold water and a cloth," barked Papa. Suddenly mobilized, Mum turned off her tears and shot into the house for water and a cloth. Dadi lowered herself to the ground beside her husband. Mona hugged her knees, her teeth chattering uncontrollably. Sunil and Mohan said nothing and moved toward each other. Mohan wrapped his arms about his little brother. This seemed to comfort both boys. It was the closest they had been to each other on this strange day.

Presently Dada stirred, twisted himself around, and sat up. "What in the name of the goddess am I doing down here on the ground?" he growled.

"You fainted, husband." Dadi's voice was soft and comforting.

"I did not faint," retorted Dada.

"Well, then, you swooned," said Dadi, determined to comfort him.

"Men don't swoon!"

"Father," interrupted his son, "you must have succumbed to all the smoke and the ashes. You know how it is with your allergies."

"Humph!"

"Just sit there for a bit until the air clears," urged Papa. "It's better already."

"Now," Papa said, fully in charge again. "It's Diwali and that's important. So let's put all these things behind us. I'll go inside and get cleaned up. Ram Lal, please sweep up out here for us. The children can help by gathering spent fireworks and litter. We have a wonderful evening ahead, and aren't we lucky to have each other, safe and sound? Dada will feel better shortly," he said, turning briefly toward the older man. "When the air is clear, you'll feel better, Father," he repeated. "I'll go inside now, so I can come back and hug each one of you." This comment was directed to the wide-eyed children.

"But Papa," blurted Mona. "Will Lakshmi come and see us now? We don't sparkle anymore." Papa cast a weary look toward his persistent daughter, shrugged his shoulders, and entered the house without comment.

CHAPTER 14

ASK MONA

"Amazing!" thought Mona as she looked around the courtyard, at the steps to the roof, and especially at the precious rangoli design. All family members, working together, had managed, in less than an hour, to wipe away any trace of the fire. Miraculously, the rangoli had been spared. Burnt paper flakes and feet running back and forth had all avoided the beautiful doorstep drawing. True, it had taken a few sharp orders from Mum, but the rangoli had been leaped across and stepped around, resulting in it being unblemished by the crisis.

The family members and Ram Lal were all exhausted but triumphant, and ready for Sharma-ji's son, Raj, to come with his mysterious surprise. Dada, now fully recovered and breathing easily, sat comfortably in Papa's great chair. Papa sat near him in a smaller chair. They laughed and chatted quietly as though nothing had happened. Mum and Dadi had withdrawn to the kitchen and were plating sweets and fruit treats in preparation for their guests. Sunil had taken refuge in a corner of the room and was playing with his new Spider-Man, while Mohan remained in the courtyard, playacting a cricket game with his sleek new cricket bat.

Then there was Mona. She had brought out her coloring book and colors. Squatting on the floor near Papa's chair, she began to color a picture of the goddess—in a rosy-red sari, of course. Tiny Lakshmi rested on the floor beside her, supposedly watching and approving of Mona's diligence.

Lights twinkled everywhere. Mona looked up from her coloring to see them shimmering on the wall in the courtyard. She could see them here in the main room too, especially those that nestled in niches around the open door. It was Diwali. Softly, again, Mona beseeched the goddess:

"Come Lakshmi. It's Diwali day.
Our little lights will show the way."

"Kyaa baat hai, Bay-tee?" asked Papa, who broke off mid-sentence with Dada. "What did you say, child?" He leaned toward his daughter.

Embarrassed, Mona stammered, "Nothing, Papa. I'm just talking to myself."

"...and to the goddess," she finished silently.

Papa paused, noting that his daughter and her coloring task were being overseen by the little goddess figure. He nodded, then resumed conversation with his own father.

"Ahem!" came a voice from the open doorway. Papa looked up to see Sharma-ji's very grown-up and handsome son, Raj.

"Come in, come in." He rose from his chair and hurried to the door. "So great to see you, Raj. How do you like living in America?"

"I like it very well. In fact, my surprise is from America. She is right here with me." Raj turned and beckoned. Out of the shadow of the great tree in the courtyard stepped a beautiful creature. With a stunning smile, she advanced to stand in the doorway. All the little lamps that surrounded the door created a shimmering radiance about her form. She actually glowed in her red sari.

"Lakshmi!" breathed Mona.

"Why, yes. How did you know?" replied a surprised Raj. "Did my father give away my secret? This is my new wife, Lakshmi. We were married in America when my parents came to visit last spring." He turned to the figure in the doorway. "Lakshmi, these people are my father's good friends. And Father's friends are our friends too," he finished.

"Come in, Lakshmi," invited Papa. "Do come in."

Whereupon, Lakshmi brought out another dazzling smile. She placed her palms together and tilted her head forward. "I am so happy to meet you," she said. "I've heard many things about you and your family." Turning to Mona, she continued, "And you, young lady— how did you know my name? My mother is devoted to the goddess and chose this name for me. My father agreed to her choice but gave me some more names too." She laughed. "But I go by Lakshmi. I like it best."

"I knew your name when I saw you," Mona replied softly. "You are Lakshmi. Your sari is rosy-red. You came to our house on Diwali." She paused. "Do you wear sari all the time in America?"

Lakshmi's merry laugh cheered Mona. "No, no, no. I only wear sari for special occasions. I wore a red sari for my wedding. That's the color for brides, you know. A wedding is a special time, and isn't Diwali a special time too? After all, my name is Lakshmi. I think of Diwali as my very own special holiday." She laughed a little self-consciously.

Mona could hardly speak for joy. Finally, glancing toward Lakshmi's feet, she asked, "Do you have beautiful red toenails like mine?"

Again the sweet laugh. "Yes, just look," she said, hoisting the hem of her sari by about an inch. "My toes are red and my feet are painted too, with red designs. It's called *mehndi*, but of course, you know that." She laughed again, somewhat self-consciously. "Are your feet painted red as well?"

Still squatting by her father's chair, Mona pulled the fullness of her frock away from her bare feet—careful not to expose the soles of her feet to Lakshmi or anyone else in the room. That would be rude. "Only my toenails. Mummy painted them yesterday, and I like them a lot." She wiggled the painted toes.

"Oh, they are beautiful. One day you may wish to do your feet with henna too ... like mine." And Lakshmi, who was wearing chap-pal sandals, wiggled her toes just like Mona had done. "If I'm around at that time, I'll help you." Then she smiled again, stepped back, turned to the others, and began to chat about the wedding in America.

Mona was overwhelmed. She again folded her feet beneath the spread of her frock, all the while thinking about red toes and red-hennaed feet. Her heart was bursting.

Having completed the work in her coloring book, Mona looked it over carefully and decided it was lovely. Not as lovely, of course, as the real Lakshmi, who by now was seated at Mum's beautiful mahogany table with the other adults, conversing quietly. Their voices floated across the room to Mona. All the electric lights in the room had been extinguished. Mum had seen to that. The only light was provided by flickering, twinkling, little oil lamps. It seemed to Mona that everything was in slow motion. Methodically, she returned her colors to their box and closed the lid. Then, in a trance-like state, she surveyed her surroundings. Sunil continued his self-absorbed play with Spider-Man. Mohan, still in the courtyard, swung his new bat again and again. The lamps surrounding the doorway took on a star-like quality, illuminating the rangoli design. Mona thought of Rama and Sita under a canopy of blinking stars, swirling downward, to land their magic chariot among lights, and fireworks, and the cheering crowds of A-yodh-ya. Her gaze moved to the group sitting and talking at the table across the room, then stopped at Lakshmi, who also stopped—mid-sentence. Lakshmi turned her head slowly toward the little girl who was still sitting on the floor by her father's chair. Her gaze met Mona's, almost jarringly, and Mona sat transfixed in her own mystical space. She felt nothing but the power and the path of that gaze between herself and the beautiful woman across the room. Lakshmi pursed her lips into a tiny smile. Barely, almost impercepti- bly, she tilted her chin in the tiniest nod. Her lips parted slightly, and it seemed to Mona that a voiceless whisper crossed the space between them, from one to the other. She didn't know what was said, but it didn't matter. Lakshmi tilted her head once more, resumed the barely perceptible smile, and turned back to the conversation at the table.

The spell dissolved.

Mona's heart swelled, nearly bursting with that unspoken, divine moment still resonating through her body. Again, she took in her sur- roundings. A quiet glow trembled throughout the room: flickering lamps and millions of glittering stars. Diwali entered, ushered in by all the light.

"Svah-gut! Welcome!

Our house is clean. Our hearts are too.

Our little lamps all welcome you!"

OF HINDI WORDS

A-ccha'	Yes / okay / that's good
A-ray bop!	Exclamation, a burst of exasperation
A-yodh-ya	An ancient city / Rama's birthplace and early residence
Bay-ta	(Bay'-ta) A term of endearment for boy or son
Bay-tee	(Bay'-tee) A term of endearment for girl or daughter
Bharata	(Bhar'ata) One of Rama's three brothers
Chap-pati	Indian flat bread, looks something like a tortilla
Chup-pal	Sandal

Chul-lo	Come on / let's go!
Dada	(dah'-dah') father's father / Grandfather
Dadi	(dah'-dee') father's mother / Grandmother
Diwali	(Diwa'li) Indian festival of lights / comes annually in October or November / five-day festival, with focus on third day—Lakshmi's day
Hindi	Official language of India
Hanuman	(Han'uman) The monkey god/a deity
Kurta	Garment, a long shirt
Kyaa baat hai	What is it? / What's wrong?
Lakshman	(Lak'shman) Rama's brother who chose to be exiled with Rama
Lakshmi	(Lak'shmi) Goddess of good fortune, wealth, piety. She is believed to visit homes where residents' hearts and dwellings are pure and spotless.
Lanka	Island nation / now called Sri Lanka, off east coast of India
Maaf'-ki'-ji-ay	A polite way of apologizing

Mehndi	Henna designs painted on body, hands, or feet
Nahii	No
Namaste	(num'-us-tay') A greeting and a farewell. In Hindi it means, "I bow to the divine in you."
Pra-saad	(pra-saad') A fruit or sweet passed to a worshiper as a blessing
Puh-TAH'-kay	Fireworks
Puja	(Pu'ja) Worship ceremony
Pujari	(Puja'ri) Priest or significant person who leads a puja ceremony
Raj	A name / contraction of raja, or king
Rama	A name / hero of the Ramayana epic
Ramayana	(Ram-ay'-ana) The epic story of the adventures of Rama
Ram Lal	A man's name
Rangoli	(Rango'li) Design, often painted on the doorstep at a festive time; signals welcome and celebration
Ravana	(Ra'vana) Demon king of Lanka

Rishi	Holy man / mendicant
Rupee	Money standard in India
Sari	(sah'-ree) Woman's garment, made by wrapping a length of cloth about the body
Sharma-ji	Mr. Sharma; "ji" is added as an honorific, signals familiarity.
Sita	Wife of the hero, Rama
Sugriva	(Sugri'va) Monkey king / Hanuman's friend
Svah-gut	(Svah'-gut) Welcome!

THANKS

To the many people who helped me write this book. Each of you is part of my life in one way or another, and therefore, part of my thinking. So I name a few here to say thanks for being my friend and for being in my life. Inspiration and encouragement for writing *The Lights of Diwali* often came from you. Any mistakes are my own.

To you~

Laurel Traye: editor and constant friend, giver of time and energy, whose dedication to clarity and excellence helped us build a book together.

Gloria Orr and Helene McInnis: honorary investors and dear friends, who made it possible to launch *Project Book*.

Pat Schmatz: author whose early critique gave me courage to move on when I was about ready to move off.

Peggy Mueller and Marilyn Turkovich: professionals in many ways, whose friendship indulged my quirks throughout our collaborations; and for permission to use a *rangoli* design adapted from the book, *Shilpa*.

Judy Patterson: friend and coworker, who helped in so many ways to craft our early outreach efforts at the University of Wisconsin, South Asia Center.

Sharon Kirk: specialist and part of my extended American family; for pushing me in the "get it published" direction.

Sharada Nayak: founder of the Educational Resources Centre (India) and all things educational, whose friendship and encouragement helped steer my work and travels in India.

Shyam Mali, Kamala and their children: my surrogate Indian family, who generously embraced me as a family member and shared their lives and holiday celebrations with me.

Lilly (Tej) Bhardwaj: my Delhi-based *didi* (sister), who took me repeatedly to Shadipur (an urban village), where we shared art activities, and where she read Hindi stories to the children.

My Family: sons Bruce and Mark, daughter Cheryl and her husband Dan, and their daughters Abby and Juli ... because I love them, and because they inspire me to "think big."

My Mom and Dad: who have moved on, but who put the floor under everything that I do.

Love you all,

-Carol

Something To Do

Use your internet

Try the key words below to find pictures to color, and more information about Diwali.

You can think of more resources to investigate. Choose words from the glossary, such as: *puja*, *sari*, or *Lakshmi*. You are creative. You have ideas. Try them, and ...

Go For It!

Suggested Key Words for Fun
(note: spelling is British)
Rama and Sita colouring page
Diwali colouring pages
Diwali colouring pages — rangoli
Lakshmi *(learn more about that famous deity)*
Festivals of light around the world *(scroll down to Diwali for activity ideas)*

CPSIA information can be obtained
at www.ICGtesting.com
Printed in the USA
LVOW12s2247260118

564139LV00003B/415/P